Hallie
the Hero

Maverick
Early Readers

'Hallie the Hero'
An original concept by Jenny Jinks
© Jenny Jinks

Illustrated by Bonnie Pang

Published by MAVERICK ARTS PUBLISHING LTD
Studio 11, City Business Centre, 6 Brighton Road,
Horsham, West Sussex, RH13 5BB
© Maverick Arts Publishing Limited August 2021
+44 (0)1403 256941

A CIP catalogue record for this book is available at the British Library.

ISBN 978-1-84886-772-7

www.maverickbooks.co.uk

White

This book is rated as: White Band (Guided Reading)

Hallie
the Hero

By Jenny Jinks

Illustrated by
Bonnie Pang

Chapter 1

Hallie and her friends loved going down to the beach after school. They splashed in the waves, cleaned up rubbish that had been washed onto the shore, and hunted for fossils along the cliffs.

"Whoa," Robin cried as she slipped on some pebbles.

"I'll help you," Hallie said, rushing over to her. But Robin was already back on her feet.

"I'm fine, thanks," Robin said. She was used to Hallie always trying to be the hero. All of her friends knew that Hallie wished she really was a superhero, with real superpowers. She was always trying to be super helpful. But most of the time her friends thought it was super annoying.

"Look, the tide's out. Let's explore the rocks around the bay. I bet we will find loads of really great fossils round there," Marcus said after school one day.

"Great idea," said Robin. "Come on, let's go."

But Hallie wasn't sure. "We're supposed to stay on the beach," she said.

"We will be on the beach, just a bit further along," Marcus said. He started to walk over to the rocks at the bottom of the cliff. "Besides, we won't go far."

"Okay," Hallie agreed. "As long as we aren't too long."

"Don't worry, we'll come back long before the tide comes in," Robin said.

Chapter 2

Hallie had never been this far around the cliffs before. The wet sand was soft and squidgy under her feet, and the rocks were huge.

The friends searched through the rock pools and along the cliff face, but they couldn't find many fossils at all.

They carried on along the shoreline.

"We shouldn't go too far," Hallie said.

"Just a bit further," Marcus called back. "We haven't even found anything good yet."

Hallie noticed dark clouds gathering on the horizon. It looked like a storm was coming. Her mum had always told her how dangerous the beach could be, especially during a storm.

"We should probably go back now," Hallie said.

"Wait, I can see a cave," Robin said. "I bet it's full of fossils. Let's just have a quick look. Then we'll head back, I promise."

Marcus and Robin headed inside.

"Wow! Hallie, you have to see this!" Marcus called.

Hallie hesitated. The tide was still a long way off. Maybe a very quick look wouldn't hurt. And at least if she was with the others she could make sure they were safe.

Chapter 3

"Whoa," gasped Hallie as she followed the others into the cave. She couldn't believe her eyes.

There, on the wall of the cave, was a dinosaur skeleton! A flash of lightning lit up the cave so they got a better look at it. It had sharp claws and pointy teeth.

"This is incredible!" Hallie said. She had never seen anything quite like it.

"See, aren't you glad we came in?" Marcus said.

Hallie smiled. This was the most amazing thing
she had ever seen.

"I still think we need to be going," Hallie said.

"No way. If this is in here, who knows what else
we might find further in!" said Robin.

Hallie was desperate to explore the rest of the cave too, but she was worried about the storm.

She poked her head back outside to check. The waves were getting big and rough, and the wind was howling. The storm was coming in quickly.

"Come on, we really need to leave," Hallie said.

"We're fine. Stop being such a chicken," Marcus said.

"You can go if you want, but we're going to explore a bit longer," Robin said. "I bet we'll be famous for discovering this dinosaur. I wonder what else we'll find."

And with that, Marcus and Robin turned and walked further into the cave.

"Wait," Hallie called. "Come back!" But they just ignored her.

Hallie knew she had to go back.

She ran out of the cave and headed back towards the beach. She couldn't help but wonder what else was in that cave. She wished she had been brave enough to stay for longer.

Maybe her friends were right, maybe she was just being a chicken.

But then a huge wave rushed in out of nowhere. It came right up to Hallie's feet and soaked her socks.

Hallie looked back. The mouth of the cave was cut off from the path back to the beach.
Her friends were trapped!

Chapter 4

Lightning flashed and thunder cracked.

Hallie was scared. She wished more than anything that she was a real superhero with superpowers. Then she would be able to fly her friends to safety. But she couldn't fly.

There was nothing she could do.

Another wave swept in and nearly knocked Hallie off her feet. So she did the only thing she could. She turned and ran.

Hallie ran as fast as she could back up the beach. She found a phone and quickly dialled the number for the emergency services.

"Please help, my friends are in trouble," she said. She told them where she was and what had happened. "Please be quick. They're trapped!"

She had done all she could. Now she just had to wait.

Chapter 5

Everything happened very quickly after that.

Hallie heard the Coastguard helicopter arrive, followed by the flashing blue lights of the police and ambulances.

She sat on the beach and watched as everybody got to work to save her friends.

The police closed off the beach, while the Coastguard's helicopter flew over to the cave.

It hovered very carefully while somebody went down attached to a long rope. They swung around in the wind. Hallie could barely watch.

Marcus was rescued first, followed by Robin.

They were safe at last.

The helicopter landed on the beach, and Robin and Marcus were checked over and wrapped in special blankets by the paramedics.

Hallie walked slowly over to her friends.

"I'm sorry," she said. "I never should have left you behind."

Robin and Marcus threw their arms around her, scooping her into a tight hug.

"We're sorry we didn't listen to you," Marcus said. "If you hadn't gone when you did, we would all have been stranded there. And then who knows what might have happened to us."

Chapter 6

The beach rescue made front page news, as did their exciting dinosaur discovery. It was all anybody could talk about.

People couldn't believe there was a real dinosaur skeleton in their town. But all Hallie could think about was the beach rescue. It had been so scary. She was just so glad everyone was alright.

The mayor decided the whole town should hold a big celebration, with a special ceremony to thank all the rescue workers involved.

The day of the ceremony arrived.

Everybody gathered on the beach for a big celebration. Hallie recognised all the people from the emergency services as the mayor called them up onto the stage. Everyone applauded as they were each given medals for their bravery. Hallie clapped and cheered louder than anyone.

Suddenly, Hallie knew exactly what she wanted to be when she grew up. She didn't want to be a superhero anymore... She wanted to be a hero in the emergency services, just like them. She just wished she didn't have to wait until she was older.

Then, Hallie realised the mayor was calling her name. He wanted her to come up on stage.

"We'd like to give a special thanks to Hallie," the mayor was saying. "For her bravery and quick action in helping to save her friends."

Hallie couldn't believe it as the mayor pinned a medal on her too.

"You're a hero, Hallie!" she heard her friends shout.

Hallie looked out at everybody, clapping and cheering for her. She might never be able to fly, but at that moment she felt like she was floating on air.

The End

Book Bands for Guided Reading

The Institute of Education book banding system is a scale of colours that reflects the various levels of reading difficulty. The bands are assigned by taking into account the content, the language style, the layout and phonics. Word, phrase and sentence level work is also taken into consideration.

Maverick Early Readers are a bright, attractive range of books covering the pink to white bands. All of these books have been book banded for guided reading to the industry standard and edited by a leading educational consultant.

To view the whole Maverick Readers scheme, visit our website at www.maverickearlyreaders.com

Or scan the QR code above to view our scheme instantly!